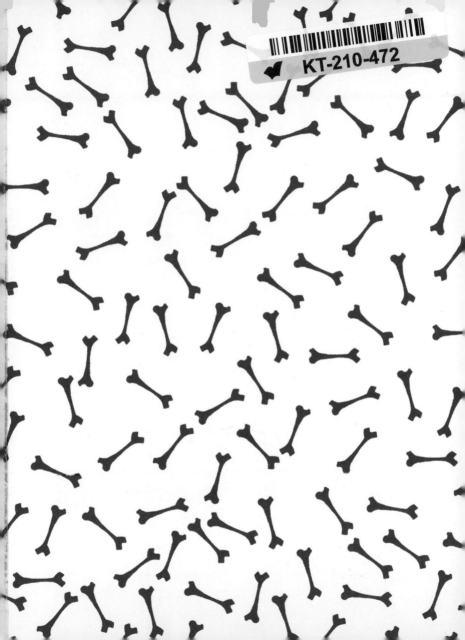

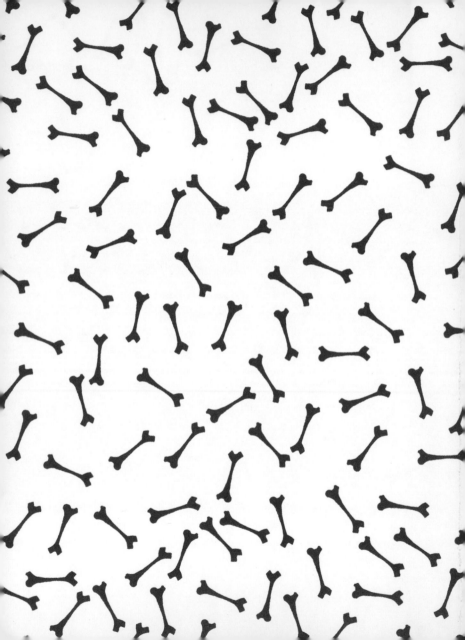

Blamehounds

Ross Collins

Barrington Stoke

First published in 2014 in Great Britain by
Barrington Stoke Ltd
18 Walker Street, Edinburgh, EH3 7LP

www.barringtonstoke.co.uk

A CIP catalogue record for this book is available
from the British Library upon request

With thanks to the Consulate General of Japan in Edinburgh for
their translation of the Japanese newspaper headlines

ISBN: 978-1-78112-392-8

Printed in China by Leo

This book has dyslexia friendly features

For Nate

Contents

1	Fart	1
2	Paint	10
3	Whack!	20
4	Eggs	31
5	Toffee?	40
6	Business	46
7	Toilet	57
8	Global	62
9	Sancho	73
10	Rumbled	86
11	Next ...	90

Chapter 1
Fart

Fart Number 1 made no sound.

The bum that was to blame belonged to Mr Lime. But as far as Mr Lime knew, only he could smell anything. He decided to say nothing about it.

Fart Number 2 made a small noise, like a mouse in distress. It was a great deal more smelly – like dead fish in a harbour at low tide.

Mrs Lime's nose twitched. She was dishing out potato salad for the children's tea and the smell did nothing for her appetite.

No one could ignore Fart Number 3. A loud noise like a car skidding on a wet road was followed by a smell like a very hot day in a butcher's shop.

"POOOOOOOOOO-EEEEEEEEEE!" Olive Lime yelled. She jumped down from her seat and pinched her nose with her fingers.

"Nobody said you could leave the table!" Mrs Lime snapped. She raised her hand to her face to try to protect her nostrils.

"Something's crawled up someone's bum and died," Gregor Lime sniggered.

"We won't have that sort of language at the table!" Mrs Lime barked. Her face turned as green as her name as the smell seeped up her nose.

Mr Lime saw his chance. He pulled back his chair to reveal a sleepy dog curled up under the table. Mr Lime pointed his finger at the dog, who had just been having a nice dream about dropping cats off bridges.

"BAD NORMAN!" Mr Lime shouted. "FARTY DOG!"

Mr Lime gave Norman a good kick up the bum with his size-11 shoes.

Norman howled in pain and then took in a big gulp of the terrible smell. It wasn't the best way to be woken up.

Norman didn't stop to find out why this had happened. He fled from the room before Mr Lime's foot could make contact again.

Chapter 2
Paint

The next day, Olive and Gregor went out to play in the back garden.

Norman watched them from a sunny spot of grass. The children had a frisbee and they giggled as they tossed it from one end of the garden to the other.

Norman didn't understand this game. It looked like fun, but why did no one run off with the frisbee in their mouth to a quiet spot where they could chew it up?

Gregor threw the frisbee higher and higher until at last it went so high that it landed on one of the window ledges upstairs.

Now, everyone knows that dogs are foolish, but sometimes they are not as foolish as children.

Norman watched as Gregor and Olive took the contents of the shed and began to pile them up against the back wall.

There was a compost bin, an old trunk, a big old pram and a stuffed anteater. No one knew why there was a stuffed anteater in the shed.

Norman watched as Gregor climbed up the pile of objects to try and get to the frisbee.

"I can almost reach it!" Gregor called to his sister. "Hand me up those big tins of paint. The ones with the wobbly lids."

Olive handed the tins up, and Gregor added them to his pile.

Norman watched as the pile swayed to one side and swayed to the other.

Then at last there was a crash like thunder and the objects scattered everywhere.

When Mrs Lime ran out the back door, she found her garden was now all the colours of the rainbow. Right in the centre were Norman and an emerald green anteater in a pram.

"BAD NORMAN!" Mrs Lime screamed. "MESSY DOG!"

Norman had realised long ago that this was his lot in life.

Norman was a Blamehound.

Chapter 3
Whack!

It was on a fine sunny day that Norman had

the cleverest idea ever in the whole wide world!

That day Mr Lime told his family that he was taking Norman to the park.

Norman knew that when they got to the park Mr Lime would meet other men with dogs. Then they would talk about more men who ran around trying to kick a football.

Norman didn't understand why these men didn't just pick the footballs up in their mouths. That seemed far easier.

But today Norman didn't mind what Mr Lime did. Norman was planning to catch up with his best friend, Ringo.

Norman and Ringo were discussing sausages when they heard a paper bag rustling. Dogs can hear a paper bag rustling from 30 miles away.

The sound came from a bald man sitting on a bench beside an old lady. The man reached into a brown paper bag and took out a large peach.

The man smiled at the peach and then bit into it.

Then a funny thing happened. A jet of juice shot out from the peach and made a perfect arc in the air. Then it dropped right down the wrinkly neck of the old lady.

Norman and Ringo watched as the old lady stood and delivered a powerful blow to the man's head with her handbag.

WHACK!

The man let out a howl as another blow hit his nose.

WHACK!

Yet another smacked across his jaw.

WHACK!

It all looked very painful.

"I know what that bald man needs," Norman said. "He needs a Blamehound."

"Sausages," said Ringo.

It was then that Norman had the cleverest idea ever in the whole wide world.

"Wait a minute ..." said Norman.

"He needs a Blamehound ... and we are

Blamehounds ..."

"Sausages?" said Ringo.

"That's right, Ringo!" Norman yelled. "We could hire out our services! This could be our chance to make the big money we've always talked about!"

"Sausages!" said Ringo.

Chapter 4
Eggs

Norman got a chance to test out his business plan the very next day.

Olive took Norman to the "Isn't Pink Just Like the BEST Thing Ever?" shop. She left him outside while she went in to get some pink glitter for her pink unicorn – or something.

Norman watched a delivery van pull up outside the shop next door. A stylish young delivery driver got out. A curtain of hair covered his eyes as he pulled a large tray of eggs from the back of the van.

He turned to take the tray into the shop and then tripped. The eggs crashed to the ground like a great eggy work of modern art.

The driver shouted something very rude and then muttered something to himself about hairdressers.

Norman saw his chance. He wandered over and began to lick up the egg.

A red-faced shop-keeper marched out
and looked at the eggy mess.

Then he looked at Norman.

"BAD DOG!" the shop-keeper shouted. Then he marched back into his shop for a mop.

The delivery driver parted his hair and looked down at Norman.

Norman put on his best "you owe me" face.

"Thanks, boy!" the delivery driver smiled. He handed Norman a crisp £5 note.

Blamehounds was in business.

Chapter 5
Toffee?

By the end of the week, Norman and Ringo had made £34 between them.

Norman had made a tidy sum by taking the blame for nasty smells and messes. Ringo had found he had a flair for taking the blame for strange puddles.

That Sunday afternoon, the two dogs lay by the swings in the park. They counted their money and watched other dogs chase sticks and harass children on bikes.

"Norman!" Mrs Lime shouted. "Time to go, Norman!"

"That's the problem, Ringo," Norman said. "The money's not bad, but we'll never expand the business while our families are around."

"Sausages," said Ringo. He sniffed something that could be a toffee but probably wasn't.

"Of course!" Norman gasped. "Ringo, my boy – you're a genius! If we got other dogs to work as Blamehounds, then we really could be rich!"

"Norman!" Mrs Lime shouted again. "We're going home. I've got work to do!"

"And so have we!" Norman grinned.

Mrs Lime's voice grew fainter and fainter as Norman and Ringo ran off across the park. Together they would find new dogs to sign up as Blamehounds.

Blamehounds was about to take off.

Chapter 6
Business

Norman and Ringo took on new dogs everywhere they could. The best places were the park, lamp-posts, and those amazing-smelling bins in the lane behind Barbecue King.

They signed up all sorts of dogs.
There were:

Alsatians

Bloodhounds

Chihuahuas

Dalmatians

Cocker Spaniels

Fox Terriers

Greyhounds

Huskies

Irish Setters

Jack Russells

King Charles Spaniels

Long-Haired Retrievers

Mongrels

Newfoundlands

Old English Sheepdogs

Poodles

Quick Dogs

Rottweilers

Scotties

Toy Dogs

Ugly Dogs

Vizslas

Whippets

Yorkshire Terriers

and Zany Dogs.

But not Chocolate Labradors, because everyone knows they aren't too bright.

Dogs were taking the blame all over town and the money was rolling in.

Prices were very reasonable. A small fart in the customer's home could be covered for as little as £3. A loud, smelly fart at a posh dinner could make as much as £20. Spills and messes were £10 to £15. Dogs who took the blame for eating homework bagged around £5, or were paid with biscuits if the child didn't carry cash.

Soon Norman and Ringo were able to stop taking blames themselves and manage the business instead. They met their workers in the park, where they took in the money and sent the dogs out to the best spots in town for blame-taking.

But Blamehounds was too big now to run from the park.

"I'm sick of doing my business in the park," Norman told Ringo one day.

Ringo frowned at Norman.

"No, no, Ringo," said Norman. "Not that business – the Blamehounds business."

"Sausages," agreed Ringo.

"It's time we set up a proper base," said Norman.

Chapter 7
Toilet

It took quite a while before Norman and Ringo found the perfect base for Blamehounds. They needed somewhere in the centre of town, with a power shower, a breakfast bar and a garden to poo in.

Sadly, as they were dogs, not many estate agents would help them out in their search. So, in the end, they settled for the old public toilets in the park.

The toilets were perfect. No one went near them any more because of the disgusting smell, which of course the dogs loved. If anyone did come near, the sound of 30 dogs barking inside soon put them off.

With a second-hand laptop and free Wi-Fi from the café in the park, Blamehounds was soon good to go.

Chapter 8
Global

Blamehounds was a hit from the very start. Dogs from all across the globe were keen to join up and to take the blame for thousands of grateful humans.

In the Arctic, Huskies took the blame for a bad day's fishing. In New York, golden retrievers took the blame for traffic jams. Down Under, dingos took the blame for burnt sausages at barbecues.

The bigger the blame, the bigger the reward. So dogs started to take the blame for larger and larger problems.

INSIDE: GLEN AFFNECK EATS BANANA WITH SKIN ON!

HOLLYWOOD ST★R

LATEST RATMAN MOVIE TANKS: STUDIO BLAMES SPANIEL

"IT WOULD HAVE BEEN A SURE FIRE HIT IF IT WEREN'T FOR THAT MUTT!" SAYS DISNAE

DISASTER!

DOG

EXCLUSIVE! SPANIEL ALSO INVOLVED IN BONE RANGER?

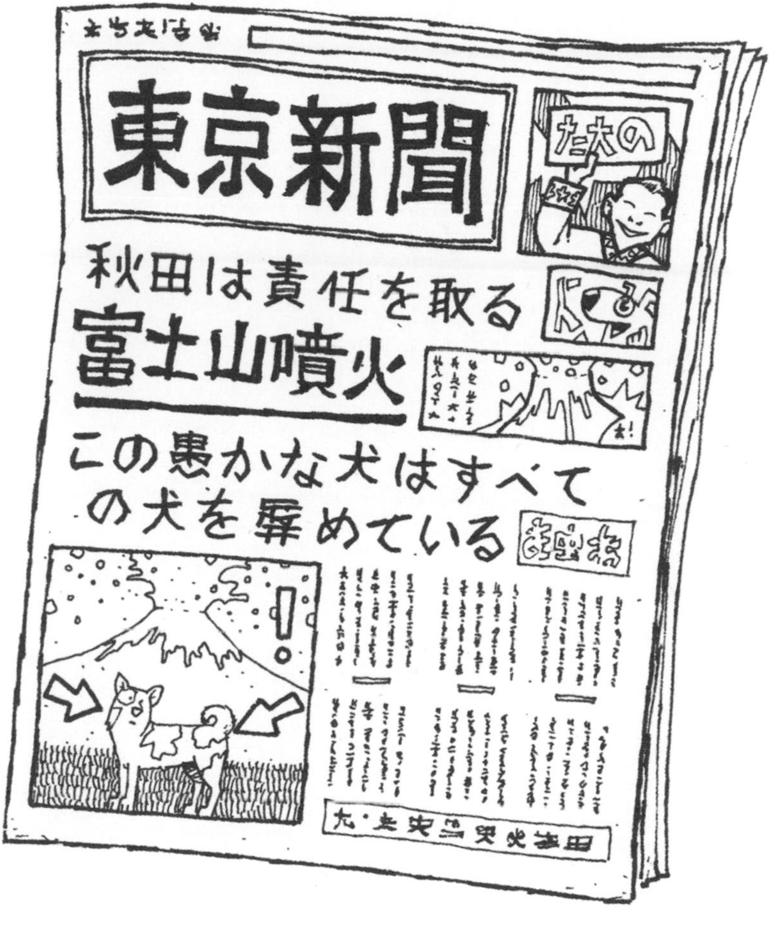
東京新聞
秋田は責任を取る
富士山噴火
この愚かな犬はすべての犬を辱めている

Blamehounds was a run-away hit.

Vans filled with luxury treats made daily deliveries to the office in the park toilets.

Norman and Ringo got big leather chairs for themselves, and chewed the arms off. When a Canadian dog took the blame for a tornado in Toronto, Ringo made enough money to buy every tennis ball in town.

"It's fine wine and bones from the butcher from now on, Ringo," Norman said.

"Sausages," Ringo agreed, as he finished off his 7th lobster of the morning.

It was all going so well.

But then one day, a small dog called Sancho took a blame too far.

Chapter 9
Sancho

Sancho was a pug who lived in the country of Tripova. For many years, Tripova had been in a bitter war with Banginta, the country next door.

Each day Tripova would send a missile over the border as revenge for a missile that Banginta had sent the day before.

Missiles came and missiles went, and everyone had forgotten who had fired the first one. They had even forgotten what they were fighting about. The one thing they did know was that Tripova and Banginta were not happy places to live.

Everybody wanted the war to be over – if only someone would say sorry for something.

Sancho saw this as the perfect blame. And he was the dog for the job.

So, one day, Sancho stepped in front of the guns – and took the blame.

The people of Tripova and Banginta were over the moon. The guns went quiet at last.

The armies of both sides lined up on each side of the border to welcome the presidents of Tripova and Banginta in their shiny cars. The world's press filmed and snapped the two presidents as they shook hands over the peace treaty.

"This is a wonderful day for the proud people of Tripova," President Smackya said.

"Indeed," said President Whackya. "At last this terrible war is over, and the good people of Banginta can sleep safe in their beds once more."

President Smackya nodded. "Who would have thought," he said, "that this small dog was to blame all along?"

"Indeed," President Whackya said. He wagged his finger at Sancho. "Bad dog!"

'With the money from this,' Sancho thought, 'I'm going to buy a butcher's shop.'

It was at that very moment that a small girl walked past all the soldiers and up to the presidents.

She tugged on the sleeve of President Smackya.

President Smackya and President Whackya looked down at her grubby face. The cameras of the world's press flashed.

"How," asked the girl, "can a small dog be to blame for a war?"

Chapter 10
Rumbled

The game was up.

People all over the world started to wonder why it was always dogs that were to blame for everything.

They began to think again about everything that had been blamed on a dog.

They pointed fingers, got into wild arguments, started punch-ups and took out court cases.

Back at the Blamehounds base, dogs got out while the going was good.

Norman and Ringo watched as their dreams crumbled to dust and their staff did a runner with all the biscuits, bones and balls they could carry.

"My dear Ringo," Norman said.

"I believe we've been rumbled."

"Quite frankly, I never liked your stupid plan anyway," said Ringo.

Chapter 11
Next ...

"POOOOOOOOOO-EEEEEEEEEE!" Olive howled.

"Something's crawled up someone's bum and died," Gregor sniggered.

But who took the blame? ...

Our books are tested
for children and young people by
children and young people.

Thanks to everyone who consulted on
a manuscript for their time and effort in
helping us to make our books better
for our readers.